FRANKIE'S FIRST DAY

To my brother Frankie

A Beaver Book
Published by Arrow Books Limited
62-65 Chandos Place, London WC2N 4NW
An imprint of Century Hutchinson Ltd

London Melbourne Sydney Auckland
Johannesburg and agencies throughout the world

First published by Andre Deutsch 1987

Beaver edition 1988

Text © Gordon K Lingard 1987
Illustrations © Martin Wright 1987

Printed and bound in Great Britain
by Scotprint, Musselburgh, Scotland

ISBN 0 09 957370 9

Gordon K Lingard

FRANKIE'S FIRST DAY

Illustrated by
Martin Wright

BEAVER BOOKS

When Frankie woke up he remembered that it was his first day at school.

He took a long time to get dressed . . .

. . . and he didn't eat much of his breakfast.

He was feeling sad
so he fed the goldfish . . .

. . . and stroked the cat.

The cat felt sad too.

"Cheer up," said his dad, "you'll like school."

"Time to go," said his mum. "Don't forget your coat."

His dad gave him a kiss and told him that he looked very smart.

On the way his mum said,
"You'll like school, there's lots to do . . ."

. . . and you've got a lovely teacher."

Soon they were in the school playground. It was very noisy.

In the classroom Frankie's new teacher was waiting for him.
She *was* lovely. "Hello," said the teacher, "you must be Frankie."

Frankie said a very soft, "Hello."

"You'll like school," said the teacher, "there's lots to do."

A girl spun past. "I'm a helicopter!" she shouted.

The helicopter became dizzy and fell on top of Frankie.

"Oh dear," said Frankie's mum.
"Are you all right?" said the teacher.

It was time for his mum to go home.

"Have a nice time," she said. "I'll see you soon."

Frankie wanted to go home too.

"Oh dear," said the teacher, and tried to give him a cuddle just like his mother. But that made Frankie cry even more.

Tom gave him his best car to play with . . .

. . . and Pamela gave him a kiss. But Frankie could not stop.

The children jumped up and down like monkeys
and pulled funny faces. But Frankie could not stop.

Vicky played him a beautiful tune
on her recorder.
But it was no use. Frankie could not stop crying.

"STOP THAT!" said the teacher.

"Stop that,"
Said the children.

But Frankie could not stop.

Soon the room was full of water.

"Put on your swimming things," said the teacher.
The children were pleased, they liked swimming.

Tom pretended to be a submarine.

Vicky put on her water
wings and a pink flowery
swimming hat.
"I'm an angel fish!" she said.

Pam was a fast swimmer

and Lee was a shark.

They were having a wonderful time.

But Frankie was NOT. He was crying more than ever.
"STOP THAT!" shouted the teacher. But Frankie would not stop.

Just then the school's new headmistress came to the door.

She had come to see what all the noise was about.

But when she tried to push open the door . . .

. . . the door would not open.

The secretary walked by. "Can I help?" she said.
"Yes," said the headmistress, "please help me to push."

So they pushed and pushed as hard as they could, but the door would not open.

The cook walked by.
"Can I help?" she said.
"Yes," said the headmistress, "please help us to push."

So the headmistress, the secretary and the school cook pushed and pushed and PUSHED until they were red in the face.

But the door would not open.

A little boy walked by.
"Excuse me," he said,
"you're not supposed to push,
you're supposed to pull."

So he did . . .

. . . and the door flew open and out came the water

and the children, knocking everybody over.

In the classroom something was happening.
A strange noise was coming from Frankie.

"He's laughing!" said the teacher.

"Hooray!" said the children.

Frankie was still laughing when his mum came to fetch him.

"I said that you'd like school, didn't I?" she said.
"Yes," he smiled, "it was splashing . . . I mean smashing."

"See you tomorrow?" said the teacher.

"See you tomorrow," said Frankie.

Other titles in the Beaver/Sparrow Picture Book series: